Why Do You Cry?

Not a Sob Story

Kate Klise ✦ illustrated by M. Sarah Klise

Henry Holt and Company ✦ New York

Henry Holt and Company, LLC
Publishers since 1866
175 Fifth Avenue
New York, New York 10010
www.henryholtchildrensbooks.com

Henry Holt® is a registered trademark of Henry Holt and Company, LLC.
Text copyright © 2006 by Kate Klise
Illustrations copyright © 2006 by M. Sarah Klise
All rights reserved.
Distributed in Canada by H. B. Fenn and Company Ltd.

Library of Congress Cataloging-in-Publication Data
Klise, Kate.
Why do you cry? : not a sob story / by Kate Klise ; illustrated by M. Sarah Klise.—1st ed.
p.   cm.
Summary: As his fifth birthday party approaches, Little Rabbit decides to invite only those friends
who are also too old to cry until he learns that others of all ages weep for all sorts of reasons.
ISBN-13: 978-0-8050-7319-5
ISBN-10: 0-8050-7319-1
[1. Crying—Fiction. 2. Emotions—Fiction. 3. Rabbits—Fiction. 4. Domestic animals—Fiction.]
I. Klise, M. Sarah, ill. II. Title.
PZ7.K684Why 2006   [E]—dc22   2005013621

First Edition—2006 / Designed by Patrick Collins
The artist used acrylic on Bristol board to create the illustrations for this book.
Printed in the United States of America on acid-free paper. ∞

1 3 5 7 9 10 8 6 4 2

For baby Milo,
who cries for 124 reasons

When Little Rabbit was almost five summers old, he made a big decision.

"Now that I'm grown up, I'm done with crying," he told Mother Rabbit. "Crying is for babies, and I'm not a baby anymore."

"I know you're not," said Mother Rabbit. And she agreed to help Little Rabbit plan his first grown-up birthday party.

"I'm having a birthday party," Little Rabbit told his friend, the squirrel. "I'm inviting everyone who's big, like me, and doesn't cry anymore."

"Oh," said the squirrel sadly. "Then I guess I can't come."

"Why?" said Little Rabbit. "Do you cry?"

"Um, yes," said the squirrel. "I cry when the others are playing a fun game and they don't ask me to play, too."

So Little Rabbit invited his friend, the cat.

"I'm having a birthday party," he said. "I'm inviting all my friends who don't cry."

"But I *do* cry," said the cat.

"You do?" asked Little Rabbit. "When? Why?"

"When I'm alone and it's dark and the shadows on the wall look like big, mean giants."

Finally, Little Rabbit visited his oldest, dearest friend—the horse.

"I know you're too old to cry," Little Rabbit began. "So please come to my birthday party."

"You're right that I'm old," said the horse. "But you're wrong if you think I never cry."

"You cry?" asked Little Rabbit. "Why?"

"I cry when I see a snake . . .

and when I get stung by a bee . . .

and when I try a new hairstyle and
don't like the way I look."

Little Rabbit returned home.

"My first big birthday party will be very small,"
Little Rabbit told Mother Rabbit. "Just you and me."

"Why?" asked Mother Rabbit.

"Because everyone else still cries," explained Little
Rabbit. "And I don't want crying at my first big
birthday party. Crying is for babies."

"Little Rabbit," said his mother gently. "I can't come to your party either."

"Why?" he asked.

"Because sometimes *I* cry," said Mother Rabbit.

Little Rabbit was very surprised.
"Why do you cry?" he asked.
"Because I have feelings, too. Sometimes
I cry when I watch a sad movie . . . or when
I have a bad toothache. . . .

"And sometimes, Little Rabbit,
I cry when I look at you."
"At me?" he asked. "Why?"

"Because you're getting so big," his mother said. "You don't cry nearly as much as you used to. I look at you and feel so proud and happy. And that can make me cry."

"But you can't cry when you're *happy*," said Little Rabbit. "Can you?"

"Mmm hmmm," Mother Rabbit said. "You can cry for any reason. Or for no reason at all."

Little Rabbit thought about this for a minute.

Then he hopped onto Mother Rabbit's lap and whispered in her ear: "Even when I'm big, I'll still be your Little Rabbit."

"Good," she said. "And even when you're big, you still might need to cry once in a while."

"Really?" asked Little Rabbit. "You won't mind if I cry?"

"Of course not," said his mother. "Will you mind if I come to your birthday party?"

"No," said Little Rabbit. "You must always come to my birthday parties."

And so they threw a big birthday party for
Little Rabbit and all his friends.
And nobody cried.

(Well, almost nobody.)
Little Rabbit felt *very* grown-up.
Being five was wonderful.